Parrots—A Favorite Pet

We may think of parrots as pets in cages, but most parrots live in the tropical forests of Central and South America, Australia, and New Guinea. A few species live in Africa and Asia. Because they are friendly and intelligent and can often be taught to imitate human speech, parrots are very popular pets. Parrots often live twenty years, sometimes fifty, and a few have been known to live over one hundred years!

Many species of parrots are endangered. Their habitat has been destroyed in some places, and some species have been brought to the brink of extinction by collection for sale as pets. For this reason it is best to buy a parrot that has been bred in captivity.

Amazon Parrots

Amazon parrots live in the tropical forests of Central and South America. They are mostly green, but many have colorful spots on their wings and heads. Blue-fronted Amazon parrots are fourteen to fifteen inches in length. They are extremely friendly and appreciate a good audience. They are great mimics with good memories and can pick up new words quickly. Feathers is a blue-fronted Amazon.

Cockatoos

Most cockatoos live in Australia and New Guinea. Cockatoos are usually white and, unlike other members of the parrot family, have a crest of feathers on the head. Cockatoos rarely talk, but are nevertheless popular pets because of their love of acrobatics.

Macaws

Macaws are large, brightly colored members of the parrot family that live in the forests of Central and South America. They have very large bills and long tails. The hyacinth macaw, a blue bird with a bright yellow eye-ring and a bright yellow "smile," is the largest of all parrots at over thirty inches in length. Its wingspan is almost four feet!

African Gray Parrots

African gray parrots, gray birds with red tails, live in the rain forests of West Africa. They are excellent mimics, not only of human speech, but of telephones, microwave ovens, and chain saws. One famous African gray, named Alex, has learned to identify many objects by name, shape, and color. Alex is reported to have invented the term "long yellow" to describe one of his treats, corn on the cob.

Feathers at Las Flores

Written by Linda Talley

Illustrated by Andra Chase

MarshMedia, Kansas City, Missouri

To Susan, my favorite talker.

Text © 2001 by Marsh Film Enterprises, Inc.

Illustrations © 2001 by Marsh Film Enterprises, Inc.

Published by **MARSH**media

A Division of Marsh Film Enterprises, Inc.
P. O. Box 8082
Shawnee Mission, KS 66208

Library of Congress Cataloging-in-Publication Data
Talley, Linda.
    Feathers at Las Flores / written by Linda Talley; illustrated by Andra Chase.
       p.   cm.
    Summary: At Las Flores Cafe in Miami Beach, the mimicry of a talking parrot named Feathers spreads misinformation. Includes factual information about Florida and exotic birds.
      ISBN 1-55942-162-2
    [1. Parrots—Fiction. 2. Talking birds—Fiction. 3. Gossip—Fiction. 4. Miami Beach (Fla.)—Fiction.]
I. Chase, Andra, ill. II. Title.
PZ7.T156355Fe 2000
[E]—dc21   00-060946

Book layout and typography by Cirrus Design

Printed in Hong Kong

1 just had this *feeling* something was going to happen today. Know what I mean? So, when they opened the door and rolled out the awning here at Las Flores this morning, I had my ears peeled, so to speak.

You may never have been to Las Flores. It's a nice cafe. Little tables in front. View of the beach.

Sooner or later everybody comes in here—fishermen, bird-watchers, sunbathers, models, even movie stars. No big deal. This is Miami Beach after all.

But it's not every place that has a parrot on the staff. I'm a parrot, in case you hadn't noticed. Joe—he runs Las Flores—brings me out every morning and puts me on my perch. Sitting up here, I've got a bird's-eye view, you might say. Not much gets by me. Or Jacinta.

Jacinta is Joe's kid. She hangs out here after school, weekends, all the time in summer. Jacinta and I pretty much keep tabs on what's going on here at Las Flores.

Anyway, this particular day I'm telling you about, the regulars were in for their coffee, sweet rolls, muffins, whatever. Olivera the patrol officer, Nick the lifeguard, María from the hotel next door, Stanley from the photomat. Jacinta and I know them all.

"Hi, Jacinta! Morning, Feathers!" Stanley says.

"G'mornin'," Jacinta answers.

"MORNING!" I squawk. "HAVA CUPPA COFFEE!"

I bet that last part surprised you, didn't it? Yeah, I can talk. That bit about "hava cuppa coffee," that's what Joe taught me to say. It's my job. But let me tell you, if you say the same line over and over again, after a while nobody pays attention. So when Joe's not around, I say pretty much what I want to say. Of course, somebody else has to say it *first*, but no problemo. People never stop talking, do they?

Anyway, this morning, I'm waiting for whatever it is I've got this *feeling* is going to happen. In walks Julio. I haven't told you about him. He takes tourists out diving off Emerald Reef. Comes in here every morning, regular as clockwork.

"HAVA CUPPA COFFEE!" I squawk.

"Morning, Feathers!" Julio calls back.

Julio sits down and looks over at Angela. She's the day waitress here at Las Flores. I wait for him to order a cup of black coffee, like he's done every morning as long as I can remember. But Julio surprises me.

"Angela," says Julio, "today with my coffee I will have waffles."

"WAFFLES!" I squawk.

Jacinta is just as surprised as I am. She gives me a look, you know, like—has Julio lost his mind?

"This is my lucky day," says Julio, and he slaps a ten dollar bill on the table. "I found this on the sidewalk. Nobody around to claim it, so I figure I will treat myself to waffles."

"Wow! Ten dollars!" says Jacinta.

"DOLLARS!" I squawk.

When Angela heads to the kitchen, Jacinta leans over and says to Julio, "You'll probably be leaving Angela a really big tip, won't you, now that you're into the big bucks?" Jacinta's a real kidder.

"BIG BUCKS! BIG TIP!" I squawk, just to let Jacinta know I'm following all this.

Later, when Angela is clearing Julio's table, she finds the ten dollar bill still lying there.

"Wow!" says Jacinta. "He really did leave a big tip! Too bad for Angela Julio didn't find a *hundred* dollar bill!"

"HUNDRED! HUNDRED! HUNDRED DOLLAR BILL!" I squawk. Everybody in the place is staring at me.

"JULIO! HUNDRED DOLLAR BILL! BIG BUCKS!" I squawk, taking advantage of the moment, you know.

This cracks Jacinta up.

Still, it isn't exactly the sort of excitement I was looking for today, so I settle back on my perch to see what the rest of the day will bring.

Mid-morning, Anna and Rosita from the marina meet here, as usual. They sit at the table right by my perch. Anna orders her Cuban coffee, Rosita her orange juice on ice.

Let me tell you, I'm about to fall asleep right then and there, when I hear Rosita say, "Did you hear about Julio? He found a hundred dollar bill on the sidewalk this morning!"

"DOLLARS! DOLLARS! BIG BUCKS!" I join in. Anna just gives me a look.

"You're kidding!" she says to Rosita. "Some people have all the luck."

"BIG TIP! BIG BUCKS!" I squawk. I like to keep up my end of the conversation. Know what I mean?

"You talk too much, Feathers!" Jacinta scolds in my ear. "All your squawking about a hundred dollars and big bucks. You know Julio found ten dollars, not a hundred!"

But I know Jacinta is not really mad at me. She could have spoken up. Right? I mean, I'm just a parrot! Who's going to believe me, for crying out loud?

But now, you won't believe this. Here's where it gets really interesting.

Lunchtime, in comes Stanley. You met him earlier. He sits down with a couple of the guys from the dry cleaners.

"You know Julio, works at the diving school?" he asks. "He got a big tip on the stock market and hit the jackpot!"

"JACKPOT!" I squawk in alarm. Is Stanley out in left field, or what?

"BIG TIP!" I add to make my point.

The guys at the dry cleaners look at me admiringly.

"That's one very smart bird," says one of them.

"JULIO HITS THE JACKPOT!" I squawk for everyone in Miami Beach to hear. The whole Las Flores crowd stops eating and stares at me. I see Jacinta standing in the doorway. She's trying to give me a dirty look, but I know she's about to burst out laughing. Then everybody is shouting and applauding and laughing at the same time.

We're talking EVERYBODY! The regulars, the tourists with their shopping bags, the fashion models in their sunglasses, the kids from the beach with their sunburns and wet hair. I mean most of these people don't even know who Julio is, for crying out loud. But we all shout it.

"JULIO HITS THE JACKPOT!" It's crazy.

Well for once I'm glad when the lunch crowd clears out. I'm thinking Julio needs to come in here and set the record straight. I try to figure out where things went wrong. I mean, all I ever did was repeat what all these people were saying.

While I'm thinking all this, Jacinta comes up to me.

"You blabbermouth bird! You and your squawking have got everybody confused. Don't you see? They think Julio got a big tip-off about the stock market and has struck it rich."

I mean, tell me, what do I know about the stock market?

Anyway, it's beginning to seem like days since Julio came in and ordered his waffles. It's the afternoon lull, and I'm about to doze off on my perch, when the big van rolls up.

Reporters and video crew climb out. Then there are more cars and more vans. I'm thinking this is the thing I had that feeling about.

"We understand someone here by the name of Julio has won the lottery!" one of the reporters calls out. "Is he here?"

"JACKPOT! JULIO HITS THE JACKPOT!" I squawk. Cameras point in my direction.

Just then, a woman with a small child at the end of each arm comes running up.

"Where is Julio Martinez? I am his wife. My neighbor says he has made a lot of money in the stock market! She says he's here celebrating at Las Flores." The cameras turn in her direction.

Just then a teenage boy pushes his way through the crowd. It's Julio's son, Luis.

"Have you seen your father?" Mrs. Martinez calls out.

"No, but I heard that he found a hundred dollar bill on the sidewalk this morning," says Luis.

24

"But we heard that he won the lottery," says the reporter.

"JULIO HITS THE JACKPOT!" I affirm.

"But I thought he made a lot of money in the stock market!" says Mrs. Martinez.

"BIG TIP! BIG TIP!" I agree.

"I'm telling you," says Luis, "he found a hundred dollar bill!"

"BIG BUCKS! BIG BUCKS!" I confirm.

Now Angela comes out of the cafe. "Well, actually, Julio found a ten dollar bill this morning," she says. "He spent it on breakfast."

"WAFFLES," I croak.

There's this big silence. I'm wishing somebody would smile at me. This is
not entirely my fault, you know. I'm just a parrot, for crying out loud. Jacinta
has slid down into her chair so only her eyes are peeking out above the table.
Then, who should show up but Julio himself.

"What's going on here?" he asks.

"Maybe you should ask Feathers," says Angela. Everyone's eyes turn on me. I mean, I've learned my lesson. And I'm hoping everybody else has too. What am I supposed to say?

Then it comes to me.

"HAVA CUPPA COFFEE!" I squawk as loud as I can. It seems the only safe thing to say. Know what I mean?

Dear Parents and Educators:

Helping children learn to use words confidently in building relationships, solving problems, and sharing information is an adventure and a challenge. During this important learning process, we must not fail to teach children that the command of a language also involves responsibility. Words are powerful. They have the ability to bring us joy, and, conversely, they have the ability to break our hearts.

Gossiping and spreading rumors are two forms of communication that are irresponsible and hurtful. They include saying unkind things about another person or spreading unreliable, untrue, or private information about others. When children get involved in this type of behavior, they create heartache for others and themselves.

The good news is that we can teach children appropriate communication skills and help them develop healthy relationships that aren't tainted with gossip and rumor. Children can learn to be sensitive to others and to use their communication skills to promote harmony and respect among their peers.

Encourage children to share their ideas and feelings about Feathers' experiences. Here are some questions to help initiate discussion about the message of *Feathers at Las Flores*.

- Does Feathers think about the words he chooses to use?
- Can words cause a problem?
- What problem came up for Feathers?
- What lesson did he learn?
- Gossip and rumors move quickly. Why?
- Have you ever gossiped or spread a rumor about someone?
- Did anyone get hurt by your behavior?
- How do you feel about gossiping now?

Work to create a supportive environment in your home or classroom where children learn about and practice honest and responsible language.

- Model language that supports and encourages others.
- Do not tolerate put-downs.
- Teach children to choose their words carefully.
- Discuss the value of respecting the privacy of others.
- Practice courage and initiative in the face of gossip and rumor.
- Encourage children to be skeptical of second-hand information.

Available from MarshMedia

These storybooks, each hardcover with dust jacket and full-color illustrations throughout, are available at bookstores, or you may order by calling MarshMedia toll free at 1-800-821-3303.

Amazing Mallika, written by Jami Parkison, illustrated by Itoko Maeno. 32 pages. ISBN 1-55942-087-1.

Bailey's Birthday, written by Elizabeth Happy, illustrated by Andra Chase. 32 pages. ISBN 1-55942-059-6.

Bastet, written by Linda Talley, illustrated by Itoko Maeno. 32 pages. ISBN 1-55942-161-4.

Bea's Own Good, written by Linda Talley, illustrated by Andra Chase. 32 pages. ISBN 1-55942-092-8.

Clarissa, written by Carol Talley, illustrated by Itoko Maeno. 32 pages. ISBN 1-55942-014-6.

Emily Breaks Free, written by Linda Talley, illustrated by Andra Chase. 32 pages. ISBN 1-55942-155-X.

Feathers at Las Flores, written by Linda Talley, illustrated by Andra Chase. 32 pages. ISBN 1-55942-162-2.

Following Isabella, written by Linda Talley, illustrated by Andra Chase. 32 pages. ISBN 1-55942-163-0.

Gumbo Goes Downtown, written by Carol Talley, illustrated by Itoko Maeno. 32 pages. ISBN 1-55942-042-1.

Hana's Year, written by Carol Talley, illustrated by Itoko Maeno. 32 pages. ISBN 1-55942-034-0.

Inger's Promise, written by Jami Parkison, illustrated by Andra Chase. 32 pages. ISBN 1-55942-080-4.

Jackson's Plan, written by Linda Talley, illustrated by Andra Chase. 32 pages. ISBN 1-55942-104-5.

Jomo and Mata, written by Alyssa Chase, illustrated by Andra Chase. 32 pages. ISBN 1-55942-051-0.

Kiki and the Cuckoo, written by Elizabeth Happy, illustrated by Andra Chase. 32 pages. ISBN 1-55942-038-3.

Kylie's Concert, written by Patty Sheehan, illustrated by Itoko Maeno. 32 pages. ISBN 1-55942-046-4.

Kylie's Song, written by Patty Sheehan, illustrated by Itoko Maeno. 32 pages. (Advocacy Press) ISBN 0-911655-19-0.

Minou, written by Mindy Bingham, illustrated by Itoko Maeno. 64 pages. (Advocacy Press) ISBN 0-911655-36-0.

Molly's Magic, written by Penelope Colville Paine, illustrated by Itoko Maeno. 32 pages. ISBN 1-55942-068-5.

My Way Sally, written by Mindy Bingham and Penelope Paine, illustrated by Itoko Maeno. 48 pages. (Advocacy Press) ISBN 0-911655-27-1.

Papa Piccolo, written by Carol Talley, illustrated by Itoko Maeno. 32 pages. ISBN 1-55942-028-6.

Pequeña the Burro, written by Jami Parkison, illustrated by Itoko Maeno. 32 pages. ISBN 1-55942-055-3.

Plato's Journey, written by Linda Talley, illustrated by Itoko Maeno. 32 pages. ISBN 1-55942-100-2.

Tessa on Her Own, written by Alyssa Chase, illustrated by Itoko Maeno. 32 pages. ISBN 1-55942-064-2.

Thank You, Meiling, written by Linda Talley, illustrated by Itoko Maeno. 32 pages. ISBN 1-55942-118-5.

Time for Horatio, written by Penelope Paine, illustrated by Itoko Maeno. 48 pages. (Advocacy Press) ISBN 0-911655-33-6.

Toad in Town, written by Linda Talley, illustrated by Itoko Maeno. 32 pages. ISBN 1-55942-165-7.

Tonia the Tree, written by Sandy Stryker, illustrated by Itoko Maeno. 32 pages. (Advocacy Press) ISBN 0-911655-16-6.

Companion videos and activity guides, as well as multimedia kits for classroom use, are also available. MarshMedia has been publishing high-quality, award-winning learning materials for children since 1969. To order or to receive a free catalog, call 1-800-821-3303, or visit us at www.marshmedia.com.

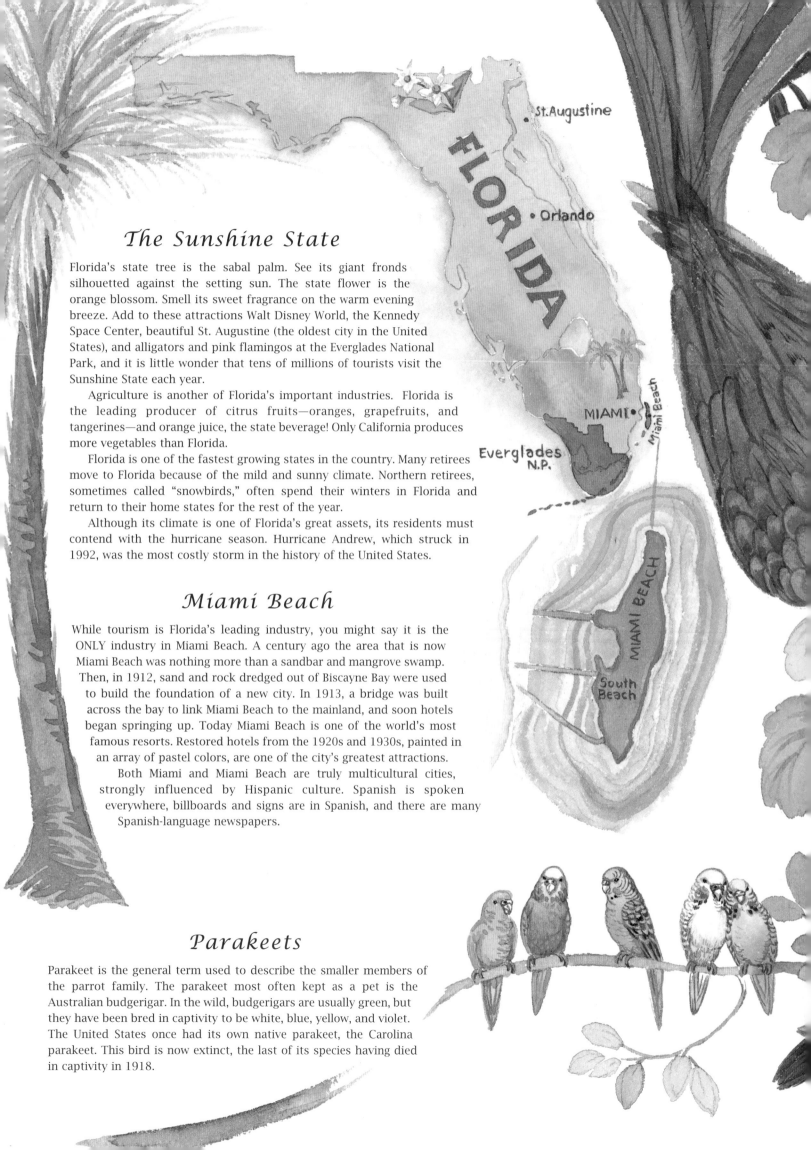

The Sunshine State

Florida's state tree is the sabal palm. See its giant fronds silhouetted against the setting sun. The state flower is the orange blossom. Smell its sweet fragrance on the warm evening breeze. Add to these attractions Walt Disney World, the Kennedy Space Center, beautiful St. Augustine (the oldest city in the United States), and alligators and pink flamingos at the Everglades National Park, and it is little wonder that tens of millions of tourists visit the Sunshine State each year.

Agriculture is another of Florida's important industries. Florida is the leading producer of citrus fruits—oranges, grapefruits, and tangerines—and orange juice, the state beverage! Only California produces more vegetables than Florida.

Florida is one of the fastest growing states in the country. Many retirees move to Florida because of the mild and sunny climate. Northern retirees, sometimes called "snowbirds," often spend their winters in Florida and return to their home states for the rest of the year.

Although its climate is one of Florida's great assets, its residents must contend with the hurricane season. Hurricane Andrew, which struck in 1992, was the most costly storm in the history of the United States.

Miami Beach

While tourism is Florida's leading industry, you might say it is the ONLY industry in Miami Beach. A century ago the area that is now Miami Beach was nothing more than a sandbar and mangrove swamp. Then, in 1912, sand and rock dredged out of Biscayne Bay were used to build the foundation of a new city. In 1913, a bridge was built across the bay to link Miami Beach to the mainland, and soon hotels began springing up. Today Miami Beach is one of the world's most famous resorts. Restored hotels from the 1920s and 1930s, painted in an array of pastel colors, are one of the city's greatest attractions.

Both Miami and Miami Beach are truly multicultural cities, strongly influenced by Hispanic culture. Spanish is spoken everywhere, billboards and signs are in Spanish, and there are many Spanish-language newspapers.

Parakeets

Parakeet is the general term used to describe the smaller members of the parrot family. The parakeet most often kept as a pet is the Australian budgerigar. In the wild, budgerigars are usually green, but they have been bred in captivity to be white, blue, yellow, and violet. The United States once had its own native parakeet, the Carolina parakeet. This bird is now extinct, the last of its species having died in captivity in 1918.